IMAGES
of Scotland

HUNTLY

The long avenue of linden trees connecting the Gordon Schools with the Castle can be seen to its advantage from the air in 1952. The foundations of the late fourteenth century stone tower house can be clearly seen in the courtyard of the Castle. The Castle Parks have altered somewhat in the intervening forty-seven years. The Show Park, opposite the Castle on the west side, is now the school games field while the upper field, formerly the playing field, is now covered with a welter of school buildings. The grandstand of the former playing field can be seen. Behind this grandstand is the 'temporary' classroom which stood for many years in the secondary boys' playground. Where the swimming pool and the premises of the Rifle Club now stand, is the primary boys' playground. Only one house (built for the police) occupies the area where the houses of Seton Drive are now situated. Of the East Parks, that bordering the cricket field is now Farquhar Road. In many of the photographs which follow, the reader will notice how less dense the housing was in Huntly a few decades ago. For example, some of the large gardens of the East Park Street houses have now disappeared due to more houses being erected in Park Street North. The old Council close can be picked out between McVeagh Street and East Park Street. (Aerofilms Ltd)

IMAGES
of Scotland

HUNTLY

Compiled by
Patrick W. Scott

TEMPUS

Tempus Publishing Limited
The Mill, Brimscombe Port,
Stroud, Gloucestershire, GL5 2QG

ISBN 0 7524 1199 3

Typesetting and origination by
Tempus Publishing Limited
Printed in Great Britain by
Midway Clark Printing, Wiltshire

Sanger's Circus parades through the Square in 1898.

Contents

Acknowledgements

I should like to express my gratitude to the following individuals who allowed me to use photographs in their possession: Dan Alexander Snr, Graeme Allardice, Nancy Anderson, Scott Anderson, Bill Angus, Charles Brander, Bill Bews, Margaret Bews, Dolly Boyd, Ian Cameron, Edna Castell, Alastair Donald, Sandy Donald, Alice Foote, Sandy Forbes, George Dow, Margaret Dempster, Sandy Duffus, Gail Dunbar, James Featch, John Fyffe, Fred Henderson, Evelyn Howard, Allan Gray, John Gray, Mary Howieson, Charles MacDonald, Betty McKay, Ian McRitchie, Mary McTavish, Christina Mearns, Charlie Monk, Philip Morrison, Stanley Munro, Sandy Murdoch, Walter Nicol, Nan Pirie, Betty Robson, Mrs Rettie, Isabella Rugg, Minnie Scott, Mary Simpson, Helen Smith, Agnes Thomson, Margaret Thomson, Alice Trapp, Jean Watt, Kimberley Wilson, the late Bill Joss, the late Norman Donald, and the late Ian Lockhart. Thanks are due also to Huntly Bowling Club, Huntly Cricket Club, Huntly Old Age Pensioners Club, and the *Huntly Express* for the use of photographs in their possession.

Introduction

t is fitting that the Square should be the subject of the first chapter of this book since for centuries it has played an important role in the life of the community. The Square was originally Huntly's market place but by the beginning of the nineteenth century the Market Muir had begun to usurp this function. The last of the important markets to be held in the Square were the thrice yearly Feein' Markets.

The area covered by the Square played a prominent part even in the life of prehistoric man as the presence here of 'The Stannin' Steens of Strathbogie' testify. When the Square exactly assumed its present pleasing rectangular shape is open to conjecture, but at least two of the present day buildings were there before 1740.

It was in the Square that Huntly folk would congregate to celebrate and to mourn. The festivities which were organised for Queen Victoria's Golden Jubilee and for the coronation of King George V are recorded in pictures within these pages as are more solemn occasions such as the proclamation of the death of King George V and the accession of his heir. Military parades, circus parades and the Feein' Market are among other events illustrated.

It will be observed that the Square has altered little since the beginning of the twentieth century. The greatest changes during the last hundred years were the building of the Huntly Hotel, the demolition of the Temperance Hotel, and the building of the new post office. Readers will also be interested in the changing uses to which the old buildings have been put to during the last one hundred and twenty years or so. Then, of course, of great interest in these old pictures are the people of Huntly themselves, many of whom have grandchildren and great grandchildren living in the town today. We see how fashions have changed; we are reminded of forms of employment which are now all but extinct; we are taken back to an era when the motor car was a rarity.

Castle Street, which connects the Square to the roadway leading to the Castle, was at one time the most important street in the town. Until the building of the turnpike roads at the beginning of the nineteenth century, all traffic passing between Aberdeen and Elgin went along Castle Street and crossed the Deveron by the old bridge behind the Castle. Photographs show that one side of this street has been altered greatly during the last fifty years (with the building of the police office for example), while the other side has remained almost wholly intact.

The views of the Gordon Schools will have many readers reminiscing about their days at the School of the Tower and the Linden Tree! Beyond the school are the Castle parks, originally the policies of Huntly Castle. A series of photographs, some more than one hundred years old, will bring back memories of a host of activities that took place here. The Show Park was used once upon a time for Huntly's Annual Show. At an earlier time it was part of the castle garden. The upper West Park has been built upon and the upper East Park, formerly the upper garden, is owned by the cricket club. The lower east parks form the Cooper Park.

Duke Street and Bogie Street have been given a section for themselves and I have included here photographs of places which lie just beyond the end of Bogie Street, i.e. the Strathbogie Woollen Mill, the Creamery, the Laundry and the Battle Hill. Similarly in the Gordon Street and Market Muir section I have included the Jubilee Hospital.

Huntly and the mighty Gordon family were bound together for centuries. The very name Huntly owes its origin to the Huntly estate of the Gordons in Berwickshire. So it is appropriate that many Gordon related pictures should be included. Huntly Castle, Huntly Lodge and the Gordon Highlanders are given due prominence.

A section has been devoted to the churches. Huntly's church used to be at Dunbennan where today there is an interesting ancient kirkyard and the meagre ruins of the church. A church at the junction of Gordon Street and Upperkirkgate replaced Dunbennan Kirk in 1727 and this church was in turn superseded by the present church in Church Street in 1805. The Gordon family was the greatest Catholic family in Scotland and played a prominent part in the religious wars of the seventeenth century. It was in the more tolerant time of the nineteenth century that a scion of the Gordon family made it financially possible to erect St Margaret's Church, whose bell tower was the first in a post-reformation Catholic church in Scotland. As well as pictures of St Margaret's, the reader will find photographs of Huntly's other churches, including the Congregational Church, which closed in 1963.

Music, sport and other leisure activities play an important part in any community and I received a very large number of photographs depicting these. Many were of sports teams, but I have had room to include only a few of these. This section will bring to mind organisations which are no longer with us such as the Town Orchestra, the Operatic Society, the Good Templars, the Townwomen's Guild, and so on.

Huntly is the centre of a wide agricultural area and indeed Huntly Parish includes a rural part as well as the town itself. I have therefore included several photographs depicting places and activities in the countryside and in the vicinity of the town.

The majority of photographs that appear in this book were taken by men and women who are no longer with us, and are now the property of their descendants. Unfortunately, some photographs that were given to me were of people or of events now completely forgotten. What a boon it would be if we could all record names of people and places on the back of each photo! Other pictures were taken by semi-professional photographers such as Mr Bertie Diveri, some of whose photographs formed the basis of several booklets about Huntly published by the *Huntly Express*, McKenzie and Co, and Harry McConachie in the early years of the twentieth century. A good number of old postcards have also been used and a few photographs originated as magic lantern slides.

One

The Square

The Square has for long been the focal point of life within the Burgh of Huntly. It is surrounded by fine buildings, some of which date back to the first half of the eighteenth century. Originally the market square, it has long ceased to fulfil that function. Towards the end of the eighteenth century, animal markets shifted to a site on the edge of the town and markets in other commodities began to die out. Feein' Markets held on the Square survived, however, until the onset of the Second World War. The Square is the place where the people of Huntly gather to mark local and national events such as coronations, proclamations, parades, funerals, galas, fetes and, of course, hogmanay!

In this view from the early 1870s we see the buildings which predated the Huntly Hotel and the Brander Library. Where the library now stands are two small shops – one was occupied by James Macleod, a shoemaker, and the other by William Slorach, a tailor. Forsyth's Lane ran behind these shops and connected with McVeagh Street. On the site of the Huntly Hotel are the house and the shop of R.R. Mitchell & Co. In the Square the fishwives from Whitehills or Sandend are selling their produce.

In 1903 the Huntly Hotel was almost brand new. In the distance we see that the Gordon Schools consist of just the central Simpson block and the small Secondary building on the left. Note the long wall, running from left to right, that encloses the 'Castle Parks', the policies of Huntly Castle. (PPC, J. Valentine & Sons)

The absence of motor cars in 1907 endows the Square with a spaciousness that is now generally lacking. The pavements are wide and flat – none of the strange present day cambers! On the extreme right is the oldest building in the Square. Built by the merchant William Forsyth in 1726, it was bought in 1897 by Mr George Arnott who established his 'Strathbogie Boot and Shoe Factory' there.

On this summer's afternoon in the early 1940s a few cars have appeared on the scene. The lantern type lamps were to disappear soon after the end of the Second World War but were reintroduced in the 1990s. The 'Millinery Saloon' was run by the Misses Duncan of Thornbank, Gladstone Road. (PPC, J. Valentine & Sons)

11

Royal anniversaries have always been celebrated in Huntly with great enthusiasm. In 1897 a whole series of events was planned to mark the Diamond Jubilee of Queen Victoria. One, which was much appreciated by the 'loons and quines' of the town, was the firing of the *feu-de-joie* by the local Volunteers. In the upper picture the Volunteers are at attention. The town band is about to play the National Anthem and when that had been done, Captain Mellis would call for three cheers for Her Majesty. This was then followed by what everyone had been waiting for – the simultaneous firing of fifty rifles! The soldiers are drawn up before the premises of R. R. Mitchell & Co. On the left is the building now occupied by 'Square Deal'. In 1897 it was the place of business of Provost James Bowman, tinsmith.

The Square is filled to capacity on Tuesday 26 June 1897, the day of the Queen's Diamond Jubilee. The Volunteers have marched away and the populace wait expectantly for the arrival of the Trades' Procession which is due at 11 a.m. No doubt they took the opportunity to admire the decorated buildings. In the photograph one can see the premises of James Cruickshank and Son, ironmongers (est. 1836). The *Huntly Express* describes this building in the following way: 'Messrs J. Cruickshank had their front festooned with evergreens, and between their windows were white shields with the dates 1837 and 1897 on them. Along the railing on the roof, small flags were displayed while a large one waved from the turret.' On the left we see the Temperance Hotel with the Royal Coat of Arms displayed over the main door. The hotel is described as being decorated with 'draperies of various colours, nicely relieved with bunches of broom.' A novelty was a transparency of the head of the Queen over the entrance of Provost Bowman's place of business. It was 'highly-coloured' and at night it was illuminated by electric light, which was itself a great novelty. The transparency was the work of townsman Mr W. J. Sim. In the afternoon 1,300 children marched to the Castle Park where amusements and a picnic had been arranged for them. Then in the evening hundreds of people climbed to the top of the Clashmach, where a huge bonfire burned, the wood having been supplied by the Duke of Richmond and Gordon, and by the local farmers.

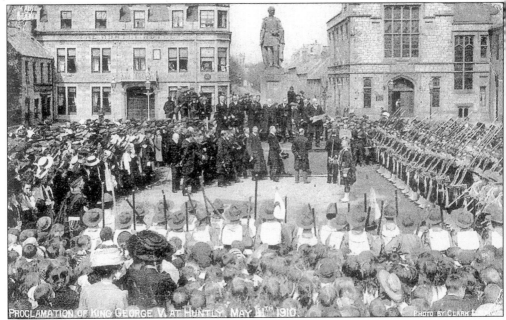

PROCLAMATION OF KING GEORGE V AT HUNTLY MAY 11TH 1910.   PHOTO BY CLARK

Royal Proclamations have always been very dignified occasions and none more so than that of 1910, when George V was proclaimed King, by Provost Rhind, from a platform that had been specially built in front of the Duke of Richmond's statue. The guard of honour was supplied by a company of Gordon Highlanders and the local Scout Troup. The Scouts, who were carrying staves, had been formed the previous year by Colour Sergeant Milton of the Volunteers.

On a cold January day in 1936 the people of Huntly again crowded into the Square, on this occasion to hear Provost Yule proclaim the accession of King Edward VIII. The schoolchildren were present with the Rector, Mr Hugh Brebner. The local Territorials, under the command of Major W. J. Murray Bisset, formed the guard of honour. In the background can be seen Gardiner's (fishmonger), the Commercial Bank and J. Brander (draper).

Whereas proclamations tend to be austere and dignified occasions, coronations are exciting and joyous affairs. So on the 22 June 1911 the Coronation Day of King George V began with the pealing of all the bells in the town. At 9.45 a.m. there was a parade of Territorials and Scouts in the Square, during which General Gordon of Culdrain presented Long Service medals to Lt Duff and to Surgeon-Major Wilson. When the ceremony had been completed, the dense crowd watched a Trades' Parade that set out from the Market Muir at 11 a.m. In the upper picture, butchers in their striped aprons are marching in front of their exhibit. The two beautifully decorated horses represent the farm servants. Among the carts shown in the lower photograph are those of Mr Donald, baker (just entering the Square).

Trades' Processions have for long been a feature of Huntly celebrations. That of 1911 was led by the Volunteers' Band. Possibly the most popular exhibit was that put on by the blacksmiths. On their cart was a fully working forge, and the horseshoes, which were made during the procession, were much sought after by the children. The procession was long and varied and was led by the tailors who were followed by the fire brigade. Then came the masons, whose two wagons showed the different phases in building a house. Next were the millwrights and then Mr Fitzpatrick's cart, upon which was an automobile 'with a very much inflated chauffeur that attracted not a little notice.' The slaters and blacksmiths followed and then came the Mutch Brothers of 49, Duke Street (see above). The *Huntly Express* described their cart as 'very prettily decorated with wreaths and festoons of flowers and evergreens.' The cart showed all the various appliances for the shoemaker's trade and bore the slogans 'God Bless Our King and Queen' and 'Hurrah For Mutch's Boots.' There were another twenty or so exhibitors that included the butchers (who had a live sheep in one wagon and a bullock in another), the gardeners, the Strathbogie Dairy, and at the end, the wagons of Mr A. Donald. His 'display was quite a procession in itself and the neatness and cleanliness on the whole evoked much admiration.'

In 1953 the Square was decorated to celebrate the coronation of Queen Elizabeth. The Robertson Fountain in particular has been made very festive while some of the buildings are bedecked with flags and bunting. The shop formerly occupied by the Misses Duncan has become 'Boyds Men's Wear.' In the background, on the right, is the Christie Park, which was gifted to the Football Club by Provost Alexander Christie in 1926.

There was great excitement in Huntly when the circus came to town! Sometimes it would be Ginnett's Circus, or Possett's, or some other. However, Sanger's Circus was the people's favourite and perhaps this was because of the large number of exotic animals which they brought with them. Here we see the elephants and camels passing through the Square in June 1898 as they make their way to the railway station.

This photograph (taken from a magic lantern slide) shows part of Sanger's parade which took place at 1 p.m. on 11 June 1898. The circus was advertised in the press as 'Lord George, the original Sanger and his £125,000 Circus Company.' There were twenty carriages of wild animals, birds and reptiles. In addition there were 'twelve monster elephants including 'HRH', the identical animal upon which our popular Prince rode when on tour in India!' There were also two herds of camels and dromedaries. Two performances were given in Huntly, at 2.30 p.m. and at 7.00 p.m. The tickets cost from half a guinea each down to one shilling. In the background can be seen the premises of Mr John Porter who, apart from being a grocer and wine merchant, was also the Postmaster. Next to Mr Porter's shop is that of William Simpson, bookseller. Mrs Simpson is seen standing on a chair in order to have a better view of the parade! In the corner of the Square is the shop of Mr William McConnachie, draper, which would soon be taken over by Mr J. M. Boyd.

The Feein' Markets took place in Huntly on the Thursday before the 26 of May, the second Thursday in July and the Thursday before the 22 of November. On these occasions the Square was full of stalls selling all manner of goods. There were sideshows and other entertainment. Recruiting sergeants would take advantage of the crowds to enlist young men (often the worse of drink) for the army. Religious tracts would be given out and preachers would address the throng. The Revd James Walker of the Parish Church strongly disapproved of these markets and in 1840 said that they were 'unmitigated nuisances'. Moreover, he declared that the farm servants were hired and dismissed like mere beasts of burden. The last Feein' Market took place in Huntly in 1938.

No doubt 'Pig Murray' attended all the Feein' Markets! He was a kenspeckle figure in Huntly who eked out a living by doing odd jobs. He lived in a room in Castle Street. The two young girls in this photograph, taken around 1895, are Nellie Ewen (left) and Olive Gordon (right). The latter's parents were the proprietors of the Temperance Hotel. Behind Olive is the shop of Donald McGlashan, baker and confectioner.

Five maids stand at the door of the Temperance Hotel in the summer of 1921. Identified in the group on the right is Meggie Neish. The Temperance Hotel was demolished in 1937/38 as part of a scheme to widen both Duke Street and Deveron Street. The Second World War put an end to this plan.

There has been a tavern or hotel on the site of the Gordon Arms since at least the middle of the eighteenth century. It was at the front of the hotel that stagecoaches regularly arrived in Huntly or departed for Aberdeen or Inverness. The hotel well deserves its name for it was at one time used by the Dukes of Gordon to dine, hold meetings with estate factors or board guests when Huntly Lodge was full. In this 1905 scene a family with luggage wait to depart.

GORDON ARMS HOTEL, HUNTLY.

In 1882 a fountain to commemorate banker James Robertson was officially handed over to the town by his widow Mrs Isabella Robertson. In 1975 the fountain was in relatively pristine condition, although some of its decorations have since disappeared, for example, the urn type finials at the corners. The central decoration under the arches of the fountain is now upside down!

In this 1908 picture, we see Cruickshank's Restuarant next to the Temperance Hotel. Dunn's shoe shop (next to James Cruickshank and Son) has a very large lamp suspended by most ornate ironwork above its door. Because of this, we find in Dunn's advertisements the phrase 'Globe Shoe Warehouse' as well as 'at the sign of the big lamp.'

In 1899 the building at the Castle Street corner of the Square was demolished and soon afterwards the building of a new hotel began. The hotel was open for business in 1900 although it was not completed due to financial difficulties until 1903. Since this photograph was taken, an extension to the Forsyth building has filled the space next to 'Square Deal.' Also the wrought iron decoration atop the tower of the hotel is no more.

Taken in the first decade of the twentieth century, this photograph shows the old houses in Castle Street which have since been demolished. A crowd of childen have gathered on the steps of the Brander Library that was built with money gifted for the purpose by William Brander, a son of Huntly who made his fortune on the London Stock Exchange. The library was opened in 1885. A horse stands patiently outside the post office, housed in a building which had originally been the Court House.

Mr Jimmy Thomson, Assistant Head Postmaster, is wondering if the mail will get delivered! Huge drifts of snow in March 1962 made all roads impassable for a time.

The old post office was demolished and replaced by the present building in 1936. Here we see Head Postmaster Mr Fred Dodds outside the post office during the same severe snowstorm.

When the new GPO opened in 1936, the telephone exchange was housed in the same building. The picture taken in 1936 shows the two operators, Miss M. A. McDonald and Miss Janet Masson. By 1959 there were thirteen operating positions. In 1972 the exchange moved to 'Balvenie' in West Park Street.

Taken in the early years of the twentieth century, this picture shows three farmers who have come into Huntly to purchase a week's supply of groceries at John Wilson's. The fourth cart is loaded with churns of milk. Mr Wilson was also the proprietor of the Strathbogie Dairy.

HUNTLY, N.B.

leading . .
igh-class
ERY,
IT,
ROVISION,
and
E ESTAB-
HMENT
capital of
ogie
nised by all
s & Tourists
tly and Dis-
so by Landed
etors, Lessees
otings and
gs, &c.
most select
ried Stock of
Qualities in
Department.
ate Prices.
ers executed
personal sup-
n. Attentive
ompt service.
ries by own
or special
gers.
Proprietor of
mous "Glen-
Brand" of the
atured Sootch
y.

FAMILY GROCER   JOHN WILSON   WINE MERCHANT

untly is every succeeding year becoming more and more popular as a Health and Holiday Resort. Gra
ry. Splendid Fishing Facilities. Capital Golf Course and Cricket Field. Visitors and Tourists will fi
lightful place for change, rest, and holiday.
ock and Price List on application. All inquiries replied to immediately without fail.

OHN WILSON, Family Grocer, Fruit, Provision, Wine and Spirit Merchant,
The Square and Duke Street, HUNTLY, N.B.

This advertisement appeared in *Huntly – the Official Guide* printed by the *Huntly Express* around 1910.

There has been a bookseller at No. 5, the Square, for at least a century. Here we see the shop assistants of 1923. From left to right: Mrs McConachie, Isobel McConachie (Mrs Kerr), and Peggy Watson (Mrs Matthews). Posters record the occupation of the Ruhr by French and Belgian forces and the illness of President Harding of the United States, an illness from which he eventually died.

The firm of John M. Boyd was founded in 1897 and occupied premises at No. 21, Gordon Street. In 1907 the firm moved to its present position on the Square. The shop has been considerably enlarged and now incorporates a carpet-fitting department. The building dates from 1736.

Two

Castle Street and the Avenue

Before the coming of the turnpike roads to Huntly at the beginning of the nineteenth century, Castle Street was the principal business street of the town and all the traffic passed along it on the way to the Deveron Bridge behind the Castle. Today Castle Street leads one to the splendid avenue of linden trees that were planted shortly after the building of the Gordon Schools. The school's elegant facade and well-proportioned tower are a memorial not only to the last Duke of Gordon and to his generous wife Elizabeth Brodie but to the architect Archibald Simpson. The avenue then leads to the old Castle and onwards to Huntly Lodge, the last residence of the ancient Gordon family in the district.

This view of Castle Street was taken in the first decade of the twentieth century. The left-hand side of the street is much as it is at the present time, but the other side has been considerably altered. Many of the old houses were demolished to make way for the new police station, which was completed in 1941. The police building occupies an area that was known as 'Fairyland.'

In this scene from 1967, a shop sign on the left advertises ice cream. Behind the shop was Huntly's only billiard saloon, now transformed into a house. The house on the right foreground was soon to be demolished to make way for a more modern structure. (PPC, Millar & Lang)

joining Castle Street to Old Road is
McVeagh Street. On the left hand side of the
hill leading from Castle Street were the
premises of William Shearer & Sons,
blacksmiths (the building has since been
demolished). In this photograph taken
round 1925, we can see, from left to right:
George Mearns, William Shearer, George
Shearer and William Shearer Jnr.

At the corner of Castle Street and East Park Street is a commodious house formerly known as 'The Anchorage.' Here until his death in 1876, lived Rear Admiral Charles Gordon, who was the illegitimate son of the last Duke of Gordon. His youngest daughter, Susan, continued to live in the house until the turn of the century. The large north wing of the house has been demolished.

There has been a painter and decorator's shop at No. 8, Castle Street since 1851. The first proprietor was Mr A. Robertson, who was followed by Mr Alexander Lobban. In this photograph, on a summer's day in the mid-1920s, Alexander Lobban stands at his shop door flanked by George Lobban and his sister. George was a well-known local sportsman who excelled at cricket and football. At cricket he was the wicket keeper and was renowned as a hitter of huge sixes. At football he was the goalkeeper. He will always be remembered for the remarkable game that he played in 1928. First Division Motherwell was playing Huntly at the Christie Park and Lobban brought off one miraculous save after another. Despite a continuous assault upon the Huntly goal by the Motherwell forwards, the first half ended 0-0, and although the final score was 3-0 in Motherwell's favour, George Lobban was by unanimous acclaim 'the man of the match.' We can see in the shop window a poster advertising a cricket match to be held in the Castle Park.

The War Memorial, at the entrance to the avenue leading to the Castle, is nearing completion in this photograph. The builders are the local firm of A. & J. Loggie, and Alec Loggie can be seen here on the lowest part of the scaffolding. The Memorial was designed by Frank Troup, a member of a well-known Huntly family.

A large crowd has convened for the service to dedicate the Memorial. No fewer than one hundred and eighty-eight men from Huntly died in the First World War, and they all have their names inscribed upon the Memorial. Also in 1921 a memorial plaque was unveiled in the Parish Church and a memorial stained glass window installed in the Gordon Schools.

Castle Street and War Memorial, Huntly.

The beauty of the War Memorial can be fully appreciated from this 1935 postcard. Here we are looking back along Castle Street towards the Square, and the Duke of Richmond's statue can be seen in the distance. On the left, partly obscured by the linden tree, is 'Glenburn', formerly 'The Anchorage' and home of Rear-Admiral Gordon. (PPC, E.T.W Dennis & Sons Ltd)

After the Second World War, a further forty-three names were added to the War Memorial. The Ex-servicemen's Pipe Band is seen here at the 1947 Service of Dedication. The band members were, from left to right, first row: W. Jessiman, J. Murray, A. Duffus, G. McConnachie. Second row: W. Dean, N. Wilson. Third row: C. Forsyth. Fourth row: J. Jessiman, J. Dunn. Fifth row: F. Taylor, J. Sutherland, W. Angus.

The Gordon Schools were founded in 1839. The fine building was gifted to the people of Huntly by Elizabeth, Duchess of Gordon, as a memorial to her late husband George, the fifth and last Duke of Gordon. The new school housed the Parochial School, the Free Church School, the Infant School and the Industrial School, and hence the use of the plural 'Schools' in the title. In 1886 the School Board got control over all the schools that made up the Gordon Schools and two years later an extension was added to the north side of the building. The above photograph was taken between 1904 and 1912, and the photograph below in the 1920s.

GORDON SCHOOLS, HUNTLY

The Duchess of Gordon chose the site of the gatehouse of the Castle for the position of her new school. The design of the building was left to one of Scotland's most prestigious architects, Archibald Simpson. Here, in a photograph taken by the late Ian Lockhart, we see famous tower of the school illuminated at night.

In 1896 a separate Secondary block was added to the Gordon Schools. From this photograph taken about 1900 we can see that the new addition was not very large. In fact it comprised a central classroom and four others. In addition there was an office for the Rector of the school and one for his secretary.

The 1896 Secondary building was for long regarded as one of the most attractive features of the Gordon Schools. Here we see the granite front of the school with its distinctive leaded windows. Soon after this photograph was taken, the building was demolished to make way for the extensive additions to the school that began in 1955.

The girls of this 1903 class seem to have been told to fold their arms and not to smile! The only scholar identified is Jeannie Grant, in the front row, third from the left.

In 1912 a two-storied extension was added to the small 1896 building. At the same time a narrow plantation of trees was laid out in front of the Secondary school and was continued along the boundary of the playground until it reached the wall of the Castle Park. A similar plantation was laid out around the Primary school. In 1999, what remains of these plantings suffers from neglect by the authorities. This picture dates from the early 1920s.

The additions to the Secondary school comprised an assembly hall, a dining room and a kitchen. At the same time a new suite of classrooms for infants was built. Some of the trees of the Secondary Avenue were needlessly cut down at this time and replaced with a large swathe of grass. The photograph shows the assembly hall soon after its completion.

The archway is a very distinctive feature of the original school building. Here we see the janitor, Mr Sutherland, ringing the school bell. The doorway, blocked in the picture, used to give access by means of a very narrow circular stair to a room occupied by the school janitor. The bust is that of the benefactress of the school, Elizabeth, Duchess of Gordon. On the extreme right, part of the fine ornamental gates can just be seen. These gates used to be closed each evening. They were damaged by a vehicle and not replaced.

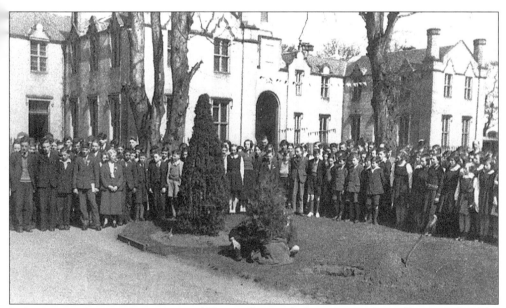

In May 1937, George VI was crowned King and to mark the occasion the staff and pupils of the school gathered in the playground to witness the planting of some commemorative trees. Miss Ewing, Mr Law and Mr Herbert are among teachers identified in the picture.

The Gordon Schools Staff, 1938. From left to right, back row: Miss McAllan, Miss Forbes, Mr A.Watt, Miss Chapman, Mr Dickie, Mr Barron, Miss Rait. Third row: Miss Balfour, Miss Stewart, Miss Jessiman, Miss Benzie, Miss Harper, Miss J. Smith, Miss Kennedy. Second row: Mr Herbert, Miss Philip, Miss Simpson, Miss McPherson, Miss McKinnon, Miss H. Ewing, Mrs Hunter, Miss H. Smith, Mr I. Law. Front row: Miss Robson, Miss Kemp, Miss Yule, Mr Brebner, Miss Jamieson, Miss Cormack, Miss J. Ewing.

Passing through the arch of the school (or 'bow' as it was usually called in Huntly) we enter the Castle Park, formerly the policies of Huntly Castle. On the right is the cricket park, regularly used by cricketers since 1889. A new pavilion was opened in 1920 by the local MP, Major Mackenzie Wood. He is the tall gentleman standing near the foot of the steps. Next to him is Mr Tom Duff, President of Huntly Cricket Club and factor to the Duke of Richmond and Gordon.

ENTRANCE GATE TO COOPER PARK, HUNTLY.

Next on our right as we walk down the avenue towards the Castle, we come to the entrance to the Cooper Park, seen here as it was in 1933. More than half the money required to purchase the park was gifted by Alexander Cooper, who had been born near Huntly and at that time was a very successful civil servant and journalist in New York. After his death his wife had memorial gates erected in his memory at the entrance to the park. Unfortunately, the Golf Club, who have come to own the park, have since removed the gates.

Public Tennis Courts and Children's Playfield, Huntly.

As we near the Castle, we see on our right the children's playing area, putting green, and tennis courts. The putting green used to be situated where the golf clubhouse now stands. In this view from the early 1930s we see three sports pavilions. On the right is the tennis pavilion, at the top of the slope on the right is the former golf pavilion, and in the distance the cricket pavilion. The latter is the only one of the three which remains (though extended with the addition of new changing rooms). (PPC, E.T.W. Dennis & Sons Ltd)

Here we have photographs taken in the Show Park on 7 August 1890. In the photograph above, the Annual Summer Show is in progress. It was held 'in a blaze of sunshine' and at times in the morning the heat was almost unbearable. There were 248 cattle and 192 horses exhibited, as well as lesser numbers of pigs, sheep, poultry and dogs. There were displays of dairy produce and of the most up-to-date agricultural implements. In the afternoon there were driving and trotting competitions and a tug-of-war. The photograph below shows the Huntly team which defeated a team of men from the countryside. The *Huntly Express* reported that 'the physique of both was grand, showing that all the bone and muscle has not become a thing of the past in these rather degenerate times.' Sergeant Aitchison (seated in the middle) captained the Huntly team.

In addition to Huntly's annual Summer Show, many other events such as circuses, picnics and sports were held in the Show Park, opposite the Castle. As part of the celebrations to commemorate the Diamond Jubilee of Queen Victoria in 1897, a picnic was arranged in the park for the children of Huntly and the neighbouring parishes. At 2 p.m. on the appointed day, 1,300 children led by Mr James, Rector of the Gordon Schools, and other teachers, marched from the Market Muir to the Show Park. As well as being fed, the children were entertained with various types of amusements that had been set up in the park. In this photograph the picnic is in progress. Away in the background, the towers of the Gordon Schools, Stewart's Hall and St Margaret's can be seen.

In this aerial view taken in 1952 we see the Gordon Schools as they were before the extensive building programme began in 1955. Cattle are grazing in the Show Park, whilst in the adjacent field the hairst is underway. The Show Park has recently undergone the scourge of development, green plastic replacing the grass that generations of Huntly folk had found quite adequate! The area now occupied by Seton Drive is a patchwork of allotments. The extensive garden of 'The Anchorage' in Castle Street is still intact. (Aerofilm Ltd)

Three
The Castle and
the Lodge

Huntly Castle is a building which is of enormous interest both from the historical and architectural viewpoints. It was the stronghold of the Gordon family who held power in Scotland at the highest level. For a considerable time it was the headquarters of the Catholic Faith in Scotland. The Castle developed from a twelfth century Norman fortress to a fortified tower house and then to the Palace of Strathbogie, whose stately ruins remain with us today. The English ambassador of 1562 said of the Castle: 'It is the best furnished of any house I have seen in the country.' The avenue eventually leads to Huntly Lodge, now officially The Castle Hotel. It was originally built as a dower house.

The avenue of linden trees leads at length to Huntly Castle, built in the mid-fifteenth century by the 1st Earl of Huntly as an addition to his tower house whose foundations are still to be seen behind this later building. This photograph (*c.* 1910) shows a road on the right leading to the bridge over the Deveron. It was closed following the 1930s excavations.

This pedestrian has followed the road above and is now nearing its junction with the wider road circling the Castle. A small part of the Castle bakehouse is protruding from the mound behind the walker. This mound was cleared away in the 1930s to reveal the substantial remains of the bakehouse and brewery. At the same time the foundations of the tower house were discovered and at the other side of the Castle the remains of the loggia overlooking the Castle gardens were unearthed.

This close-up of the beautiful oriel window high up on the great round tower of the Castle was taken in 1897. The Castle was badly damaged in 1594 and the oriel window was part of the reconstruction and embellishment of the building carried out by the first marquis. The heraldic doorway and fireplaces were also added at this time. The built-over window at the bottom of the picture was opened up in the 1930s.

This is perhaps the earliest drawing of the Castle in existence and is said to date from 1743. Hanoverian troops used the Castle as a barracks after the 1745 rebellion. When the troops departed, the Castle was left to decay. To the right of the Castle can be seen some farm buildings and hayricks.

Children's Beach and Swimming Pool, Huntly.

Near the Castle is the shingle beach on the River Deveron where generations of local children have paddled and swum. The pool of water below the beach is the Basin or Horse Pot. (PPC, E.T.W. Dennis & Sons)

The winter of 1947 is well remembered for its severity. Long stretches of the Deveron were completely frozen from bank to bank. William and Stanley Alexander of the 'Firs', Kinnoir, are standing in the very middle of the river opposite the shingle beach near the Castle.

Twenty-five years earlier, cattle were grazing on the banks of the Deveron. They helped to keep short the part of the Castle Park used by the local golfers.

Above: Behind the Castle is the old bridge crossing the Deveron. Before the coming of the turnpike roads, the main route to Elgin crossed this bridge. The fine avenue of trees leads to Huntly Lodge, which was constructed by the Duchess Katherine in 1756. (Photograph by Mr Bertie Diveri, *c.* 1900)

When Elizabeth Brodie married George, Marquis of Huntly in 1813, the couple decided to make Huntly Lodge their main residence. When George became Duke of Gordon, they resided at Gordon Castle, Fochabers. On the sudden death of her husband in 1836, Elizabeth returned to the Lodge where she continued to reside until her death in 1864. The Lodge, seen here in 1903, was then let to a series of tenants who included Michael Hughes from Lancashire and Colonel Cumberland and his wife Laura, Lady Grant. In 1924 it was sold to Mr (later Sir) Leybourne Davidson, whose family had made a fortune from tea and rubber plantations. During the Second World War the Lodge was requisitioned by the Government in order to provide accommodation for officers. Large field guns camouflaged with nets lined the Lodge Avenue. In 1946 it became 'The Huntly Castle Hotel.' (PPC, J. Valentine & Sons)

Below opposite: A bridge has crossed the River Deveron at this point at least since the early part of the seventeenth century. On a map published by John Blaeu in his Atlas Novus of 1654, the bridge is clearly marked. This photograph showing the picturesque span of the bridge was taken between 1900 and 1905.

Elizabeth, Duchess of Gordon was a keen horticulturist. When the Strathbogie Horticultura Society was founded in 1846, Her Grace, along with Mrs Bisset of Lessendrum, agreed to become a patroness. When, as Marchioness of Huntly, she made Huntly Lodge her main residence, she ordered that the gardens be enlarged and redesigned. Alas the gardens have now largely disappeared, but something of their beauty has been captured in this old photograph taken in 1892

In Huntly Lodge Grounds, Huntly

The formal garden was designed as a huge basket of flowers. There was a walled garden of about three acres tastefully laid out with an upper terrace sheltered by flowering shrubs. In addition there was a rock garden, a rose garden, wide lawns with tennis courts and so on. When the Duchess of Gordon had completed her walk through her garden she would as often as not betake herself to the timber 'Tea House.' No trace of this building remains.

Four
Duke Street and Bogie Street

BOGIE STREET, HUNTLY

Together these streets were formerly called Bogie Wynd. Mr George Gray, writing about conditions in the 1820s, informs us that from Church Street to MacDonald Street on the west side, there was not one slated building. All were thatched. On the east side there were slated buildings at each end 'with long dead garden walls intervening.' Although the west side has completely altered, the east side would be easily recognisable to Mr Gray. Bogie Street eventually leads to the Bogie Bridge. At one time the bridge was so steeply arched that horses had often to be unhitched and the carriages manhandled over the steep gradient. The date 1807 can be seen carved into the bridge's side. At this time the old arched bridge was demolished and a new one built to accommodate the turnpike road that had just reached Huntly.

Until the Bypass was built in 1978, Duke Street and Bogie Street formed part of the main road between Inverness and Aberdeen. The narrowness of the former resulted in frequent traffic jams in the 1960s and 70s. However, in 1905 the street was bereft of traffic of any kind! The clock on the right of the street marks the position of the premises of Watt, jeweller. The wheel on the left is advertising Fitzpatrick's cycle shop.

The shopkeepers on this bright summer's morning in the 1920s have lowered their sunshades over the shop windows. Looking up Duke Street towards the Square, the Temperance Hotel can be seen in the distance. On the right of the photograph, the Royal Oak sign advertises stabling.

In 1882 the *Huntly Express* moved to premises at 18-22 Duke Street and remained there until 1985. This photograph shows the original staff of the *Express*. From left to right, back row: J. M. Stobie, Joe Dunbar, A. M. Braik and A. Mitchell. Front row: R. Stobie, Adam Dunbar, G. Scott and A. B. J. Kelman. Adam Dunbar founded the paper. When Adam retired in 1888, his son Joe became the proprietor.

Huntly Express

STRATHDEVERON, STRATHBOGIE AND STRATHISLA ADVERTISER.

No. 1.	HUNTLY, SATURDAY, AUGUST, 15, 1863.	PRICE 1d.

LOST, on the evening of Tuesday, the 11th inst., between Dunscroft and Huntly, A BROWN SILK UMBRELLA, with Glazed Cover. Whoever will bring the same to the Office of this Paper, will be Rewarded.

SALE OF GROWING CROP.

THERE will be exposed for Sale by Public Roup at WAULKMILL, Parish of Kennethmont, belonging to James Gordon, on Thursday, 20th Aug. curt., the whole growing Crop on said farm. To be put up in Lots to suit Purchasers.

Sale to Commence at 12 o'Clock, noon
JAS. M'KINNON, Auctioneer.
Waulkmill, 10th August, 1863.

SALE OF GROWING CROP.

THERE will be exposed for Sale by Public Roup, at WARDHOUSE, Parish of Kennethmont, on Saturday, 29th Aug. curt., from 35 to 40 Acres of Corn. In Lots to suit Purchasers.

Sale to commence at 12 o'clock.
JAS. M'KINNON, Auctioneer.
Wardhouse, 14th August, 1863.

J. BOWMAN,
PLUMBER, BRASSFOUNDER AND FINISHER, BELL-HANGER, WHOLESALE COPPER AND TINSMITH,

EXECUTES all sorts of Brass Castings, and has always on hand a large Stock of Sheet Lead and Zinc, Ridges, Planks, &c. Also, Perforated Sheet Zinc for Thrashing Mills— 1-16th thick. Gas Brackets and Finishings kept in Stock, and also made up to order to any pattern.

WINCEYS, FLANNELS, & BLANKETS,
AT LAST YEAR'S PRICES.

Notwithstanding the very great advance on Wools,
WILLIAM WEBSTER,
has been fortunate in securing upwards of ONE HUNDRED AND TWENTY PIECES OF WINCEY, and a corresponding quantity of FLANNELS AND BLANKETS, all
At Last Year's Prices.
W. W. having made his purchases before the advanced prices of Wools were fixed for the present year, he can with confidence recommend these Goods, being well-finished and Cheap.
GORDON ST., HUNTLY.

GEO. GRAY,
MEADOW STREET, HUNTLY,
VALUATOR OF BUILDINGS, &c.

WOULD direct attention to his Stock of SUMMER and AUTUMN GOODS, at the undernoted prices:—

LADIES'
Kid Elastic Boots, 7s 6d, 10s 6d, and 12s 6d.
Ladies' Balmorals, 3s 6d, 4s 6d, 5s, 7s 6d, 8s 6d.
Slippers from 1s 10d, Shoes, stout and light, from 5s 6d.

GENT.'S BOOTS.
Elastic Sides, 9s 6d, 10s 6d, 12s 6d, 13s 6d, &c.
Balmorals, 8s 6d, 10s 6d, 12s 6d.
Bluchers, 6s, 6s 6d, 8s 6d, 9s 6d, 10s 6d.

THE
CHEAPEST MUSIC EVER PUBLISHED.
FOR THE PIANOFORTE.

Observe:—All the Nos. of Boosey's Musical Cabinet, and Chappell's Musical Magazine, kept constantly in Stock, by
A. DUNBAR & SONS,
SQUARE, HUNTLY.

BOOSEY'S MUSICAL CABINET,
A Library of Vocal, Pianoforte, and Dance Music, in Shilling Books.
NOTICE—*The whole of the Songs have Pianoforte Accompaniments and English Words.*
CONTENTS

1. Twenty Songs by Mendelssohn, 1s.
2. Twelve Songs by Balfe, 1s.
3. Fourteen Songs by Verdi, 1s.
4. Twenty Christy's Minstrels' Songs (1st Selection), 1s.
5. Fifty Popular Waltzes, 1s.
6. Twelve Sets of Quadrilles, 1s.
7. Fifty Polkas and Galops, 1s.
8. Twenty-Five Gems by Verdi, for Piano, 1s.
9. Nine Original Pianoforte Pieces, by J. Asher, 1s.
10. Ten Nocturnes and Mazurkas de Salon for Pianoforte, by Goria, Talexy, Wely, and Cramer, 1s.
11. Twelve Drawing-Room Pianoforte Pieces, 1s.
12. Fifteen Songs by Beethoven, 1s.
13. Twelve Songs by Hatton and Linley, 1s.
14. Twenty Ballads by Popular Composers, 1s.

ski.—Beethoven's Sonata No. 1. Op 14, E.—Beethoven's Sonata, No. 2, Op. 14, G. Complete. 1s.
50. Beethoven's Sonata, Op. 22, B flat. Dedicated to le Comte de Browne.—Beethoven's Sonata with Funeral March, Op. 26. Dedicated to Prince Lichnowski. Complete, 1s.
51 Beethoven's Sonata Quasi Una Fantasia, No. 1, Op. 27, C Minor. Dedicated to the Countess Giulietta di Giucciardi. (Known as the Moonlight Sonata).—Beethoven's Sonata Quasi Una Fantasia, No. 2, Op. 27, E flat. Dedicated to the Princess de Lichtenstein. Complete, 1s.
52 Beethoven's Sonata Pastorale, Op. 28, D. Dedicated to M. de Sonnenleis.—Beethoven's Sonata, No. 1, Op. 31, G. Complete, 1s.
53. Beethoven's Sonata No. 2, Op. 31, D minor. Beethoven's Sonata No. 3, Op. 31, E flat. Complete, 1s.
54. Beethoven's Sonata, No. 1, Op. 49, G minor. Beethoven's Sonata, No. 2, Op. 49, G.—Beethoven's Sonata, Op. 53, C. Dedicated to Count de Waldstein. Complete, 1s.
55. Beethoven's Sonata, Op. 54, F.—Beethoven's Sonata Appasionata, Op. 57, F minor. Dedicated to Count de Brunswick. Complete, 1s.
56. Beethoven's Sonata, Op. 78, F Sharp. Dedicated to Madame la Comtesse de Brunswick.—Beethoven's Sonata, Op. 79, G.—Beethoven's Sonata Caracterisque, Op. 81, E flat. Dedicated t othe Archduke Rtolophte. Complete, 1s.
57. Beethoven's Sonata, Op. 90, G minor. Dedicated to Count Maurice Lichnowski,

The first issue of the *Huntly Express*, dated 15 August 1863.

Above: When the business of Alexander Donald, baker, was sold in 1997, a link with the past was severed for the bakery had served the community for 135 years. The founder, Alexander Donald, stands in the middle of this group. The lady to the right is Elsie Mellis, and the baker with the dog is Alexander Donald Jnr. The son and grandson of the latter, both named Alexander Donald, would inherit the business.

Duke Street, Huntly.

Here in 1929 or 1930, we view Duke Street from the Royal Oak. Mr John Davidson in a white apron is standing at the entrance to his chemist's shop. This building was once home to the grandmother of George MacDonald, while the adjacent house was the birthplace in 1824 of the author himself. Two years later the family re-moved to the farm of Upper Pirriesmill. Next to the chemist's shop is that of shoemaker John A. Dunn, whose place of business had formerly been situated on the Square. Then came the premises of John Singer (confectioner) and of James MacKenzie and Co. (booksellers and stationers). The small shop of Miss Morgan (fancy goods and needlework) was next and then the residence of Dr Ogg. Beyond the Doctor's house was the shop of Miss Burns (milliner). Opposite Davidson's is the cycle shop of Robert (Bob) Whyte.

Below opposite: This view (*c.* 1900) has been taken at the point where Old Road and Church Street meet Duke Street. On the right is the Royal Oak, built in 1726 by William Petrie, who is described as a 'burgess of Huntly.' The Royal Oak is referred to in George MacDonald's novel *Robert Falconer*, first published in 1868.

In this postcard dated July 1942, we see the premises of J. B. Singer, confectioner, and of McKenzie & Co., stationers. Further along the street is the famous '49' sign of Mutch Brothers, shoemakers. At the bottom of the hill is the ornate building complete with balcony, which was constructed in 1907 by the well-known Huntly firm, A. & J. Loggie. (PPC, M. & L. National Series)

This view of Duke Street, dating from around 1910, has been taken at the point where the street changes its name to Bogie Street. The old established firm of Dawson & Co., draper, occupied the whole building. Upstairs worked the milliners and dressmakers. Next door is the butcher's shop of James Scott and beyond, the well-known facade of Mutch Brothers.

The above photograph shows Bogie Street around the year 1900. Three buildings on the right have their gables facing the street. The middle one is thatched. Various materials seem to have been used for thatching, including heather. This building has now been heightened. Between the first two of these buildings a close led to the stables of Wordie & Co., who carried on a considerable carting business for the railway company. The nearest of the buildings was used by Wordie's as an office. The photograph below was taken about ten years later. Note that the thatched roof has now been slated. Over the entrance to the yard, next to Wordie's office, a sign has been erected by William Boddie and Co., monumental masons. The large shop on the nearer side of Boddie's yard was that of Alec 'Beardie' Dufton. Alec was a grocer who made and sold his own jam and also bottled his own whisky.

Wordie's kept about seven horses in their Bogie Street stable. One of the firm's best known carters was Sandy Nicol. Sandy is making a delivery in 1947 to the schoolhouse in Deveron Road.

Until the early 1940s, George Innes' popular fish restaurant stood opposite the Strathbogie Hotel. It is described by those who remember it as a rather ramshackle building. It was partly timber in construction and it is not all that surprising that it burnt down. Mr Innes then opened a chip shop in Castle Street.

Housewives queue to collect their milk from the churns on the milkman's cart. Rose Cottage behind them and the view of Old Road have scarcely altered since this picture was taken in the early years of the twentieth century. However, the granite setts have long given way to tarmacadam.

Carters carrying supplies regularly visited the parishes in the neighbourhood of Huntly. Here we see Jimmy Thomson and his horse Prince in the mid-1950s, loaded up and ready to make the journey to Glass or Rothiemay. Jimmy worked for A. B. Yule, general merchant and is photographed outside the firm's premises, which extended from Bogie Street along Queen Street.

Bogie Street terminates at the Bridge of Bogie, seen here in an old photograph dating back to 1892. The bridge is much narrower than at the present time. In the foreground a man is wending his way home after gathering wood, presumably from the Battle Hill. Slightly farther on, a group of women in white aprons are having a break from their work in the mill. The tall chimney on the left background is that of the Gas Works in Gladstone Road.

Finished articles of all sorts were produced at the mill both for the home market and for export. One of the employees, Mrs Johnston, is seen here operating the glove-making machine.

Bogie Bridge, Huntly

Cloth was woven in the mill beside the Bridge of Bogie since the late eighteenth century. During most of that time the business, the Strathbogie Woollen Company, was owned by the Stephen family of Huntly. The mill, which was powered by both steam and water, closed in 1954 and has since been demolished.

Another of the mill employees, Miss Jean MacIntosh, glove-fingerer, concentrates on completing the article.

Looking upstream from the Bridge of Bogie in 1920, the observer could not fail to see the salmon ladder that allowed the leaping fish easier access to the top of the falls. The river has now altered its course slightly with the result that the ladder is no longer in use. On the extreme right can be seen part of the Huntly Dye Works.

In times of storm, the level of the river Bogie can rise to an astonishing degree. The placid stream then becomes a raging torrent. Such was the case on the 8 August 1930, as can readily be seen in this photograph. The water has breached its banks and is flooding both Stephen's Mill and Huntly Dye Works.

untly Dye Works was part of Stephen's Mill til it was bought by Mr John Castell. The uilding here shows the date 1872, but a eworks had stood on the site since the end of e eighteenth century. Mr Alex Castell and s son William stand at the doorway of their ace of business in 1925. The Dye Works ased to operate during the Second World /ar, and the building was used for a time as a oys' club before being demolished when a new wer was installed.

A few hundred yards downstream stood Huntly's oldest mill, the Mill of Huntly, which closed in the early 1940s. In this photograph taken around 1905, both the meal mill and the sawmill can be seen. A favourite walk for Huntly folk was over the wooden bridge in front of the mill and then upwards past Piriesmill to the Battle Hill. The introduction of barbed wire fences and a silage pit has made this walk well-nigh impossible.

When we cross the Bridge of Bogie we find ourselves in the parish of Drumblade. Immediately on our right is the entrance to Huntly Railway Station. The Great North of Scotland Railway came to Huntly in 1854, though it took another four years for the line to reach Inverness. Looking along the line in the direction of Aberdeen, we see the station as it was c. 1910.

The coming of the railway to Huntly in 1854 meant that goods of all sorts could be transported to and from the town with a rapidity hitherto impossible. When the internal combustion engine arrived on the scene, the roads began to usurp business from the railway. Coal and other bulky goods, however, continued to arrive at Huntly's goods yard. Here we see in 1959, Huntly coalman Jimmy Featch with his horse Nell, collecting a load of coal.

Many a traveller, before boarding the train, first visited the kiosk of John Menzie & Co., where he bought the daily paper, chocolate or perhaps cigarettes. Almost certainly he would have been served by Miss Bella Whitecross, who worked in the kiosk for fifty-one years. She is seen here in 1952, just before her retirement.

In 1952 some of railway workers were awarded with long service medals. Provost Barron of Huntly visited the station and made the awards. In the photograph taken on the occasion, the following have been recognised. From left to right, back row: -?-, Dod Duncan, Jimmy Nicol, Bill Grant. Front row: Geordie Matheson, Gavin Horn, Provost Barron, -?-, George Bailey (Station Master, 1943 to 1962).

Beyond the railway beside Thane's Burn stood Huntly Laundry Ltd, of which not a vestige remains. Founded in 1907, it finally closed its doors in 1969. The green and yellow laundry vans were a familiar sight in the north east of Scotland. In this photograph driver Bill Angus stands beside his new van on the outskirts of Keith.

The laundry building was by no means a very pretentious one, being almost entirely made of green painted corrugated iron. In 1937, Miss Helen (Nell) Gray is taking the Alsatian, Judy, for a walk past the laundry.

Near the laundry was situated Huntly Creamery, which began life as The Northern Creameries in 1897. By 1930 the business was owned by George Mellis & Son Ltd, the wholesale grocers. On the extreme right is Sandy Nicol and next to him is the manager Tom Watt, who played the church organ and conducted the Male Voice Choir and Town Orchestra.

At one time a favourite stroll for Huntly folk took the walker past Yule's Meal Mill, through the white gates and then by *The Farm*, the laundry, the creamery, the mart and back by the 'gullet.' In this card sent on 8 September 1910, three girls are approaching the creamery from *The Farm*.

As the walker leaves Bogie Street and the railway bridge behind him, he comes to a road on his left which leads to the Battle Hill. On the lower slope of this hill in the nineteenth century, the well-to-do had mansions built for themselves. In the above photograph taken soon after the dawn of the twentieth century, the five large houses are seen. The house on the left at the back was named *Maryfield* by grocer John Porter, after his wife Mary Sellar. The house on the right at the back was built by a navy man, Commander Simpson, and called *Dalhousie*. Moving to the lower row of houses, we have on our left *The Battlehill House*, which was built by a Mr Dunn, whose monogram decorates the building. This house became the home of the Sellar family. The middle house was the home of Colonel Mellis and rather confusingly named *Battlehill House*. The house on the right was built by the Sellar family and named *Aldie House* after a small Ross-shire estate which was owned by the family. The photograph below shows Col. Mellis' house shortly after it was built in 1887.

Five
Gordon Street and the Market Muir

GORDON ST. SHOWING TOWN HALL, HUNTLY.

Gordon Street is named after Alexander, fourth Duke of Gordon. He succeeded to the title in 1752 and was an extremely popular landowner. When times were hard he could be relied upon to fill the Huntly girnels with meal. He died in London in 1827. The funeral cortege travelled northward in easy stages reaching Huntly six weeks after it had set out from London. It passed along Gordon Street on its way to the Parish Kirk. Indeed Gordon Street has witnessed many processions and perhaps the most spectacular of these was that organised to celebrate the coronation of King George V in 1911. The exhibitors gathered in the Market Muir and then paraded along Gordon Street until they reached the Square.

Gordon Street is dominated by the splendid hall with the clock tower that was built in 1875 with funds left to the town by Alexander Stewart, who had been procurator fiscal in Huntly. Behind the tree on the left can be glimpsed the bank building designed by the architect Archibald Simpson. Completed in 1842 it has continued in use as a bank to the present day. The tree and others around the Square were cut down in 1998 when just reaching maturity.

Archibald Simpson's bank was one of the illustrations which appeared in the catalogue issued in 1936, when the feus of 1131 houses, 9 hotels, 117 shops, 21 factories, 5 churches, 3 hospitals, 6 halls, 3 manses, 6 banks and other buildings were sold. Also sold were the 68 farms and small holdings together with fishing rights, water rights, quarries, allotments etc., which comprised the 12,142 acres of the Huntly Estate. The estate had been the property of the Duke of Richmond and Gordon.

Gordon Street is here viewed (*c.* 1910) from the point where it intersects with Upperkirkgate and Torry Street. On the left is the shop of Alexander Gordon with its well-known eagle decoration above the door. Mr Gordon as a young man worked for the firm of George Mellis & Son before going into business on his own around 1874. Mellis' office is opposite Mr Gordon's shop.

By the 1960s, Alexander Gordon's shop had expanded to annex the neighbouring building, which had at one time been the place of business of Mrs Calder, pawnbroker. Jimmy Featch the coalman is striding past the shop while Police Sergeant Smart and one of his constables look on.

When Stewart's Hall was built, a room was set aside for use as the Council Chamber. Unfortunately the Town Council was abolished in 1975. The photograph shows Huntly's last Council. From left to right, back row: Ian Carnegie, Robert Ness, Nigel Henderson, Ian Archibald(Burgh Surveyor), Ian Milne, William Watson, Stanley Jenkins, Albert Rough(Hall Keeper). Front row: Baillie James Cullen, John Christie (Town Clerk), Provost Reid Flory, Baillie William Steven, John Boyd.

This view from Stewart's Hall is reckoned to have been taken around 1930. In the foreground are the buildings that lie behind the Gordon Arms and the Temperance Hotel. The Strathdeveron Hotel on Deveron Street can be seen. In the background is St Margaret's Church and School.

Looking from the same vantage point some twenty years earlier, we see in the foreground Richmond Lane and Granary Street. The old granary at this time was used by Messrs Sellar. It is believed that much of the material which was used to build the Granary was taken from Huntly Castle. In earlier times, meal had been stored in large girnals kept inside the Tolbooth that stood on the Square in front of the Gordon Arms. The main part of Sellar's factory is on the right (with the tall chimney.) The Parish Church and Strathbogie Church can also be discerned. In the distance are the Battle Hill and the Ba Hill.

73

The firm of George Sellar & Son had its origins in Huntly in 1822. With the invention of the moveable point plough, the firm's fame spread throughout the kingdom and a flourishing overseas trade was developed in the 1870s. This view of their Granary Street factory is from around 1900. In 1915 the main production plant moved to Alloa. In 1976 the old factory was closed and a new one built in the Huntly Industrial Estate.

The workers of the Sellar's factory take time off to have their photograph taken in 1922. Two men have been identified. In second row from the back (with seven men in it), Tom Henderson is on the extreme left and Eddie Farquharson is fourth from the left.

Domenico Rizza set up shop in Huntly at No. 16, Gordon Street in 1929 and is seen here at his shop door soon afterwards. The firm, now known as James Rizza and Sons, still occupies the same premises (though much altered.) Ice cream is made at their factory in Upperkirkgate and is sold throughout the country.

Lady Davidson of Huntly Lodge leads the Red Cross contingent in this 1944 wartime parade along Gordon Street. Immediately behind Lady Davidson is Nora Rae. On the right of the first rank is Andrea Thomson. On the right of the last rank of three is Margaret Dempster. Following on behind are the Land Girls, while on the right is the large illuminated sign of the Playhouse (though it remained unlit during the war years).

Above: In 1897 the premises of the firm of William Niven were at No.27, Gordon Street. Later they moved to No. 11, Gordon Street until finally settling at No. 37. Two fishwives stand beside the window. A little boy on the left has failed to stand still during the lengthy exposure required for the photograph and as a consequence appears to have three heads! No. 27 was later the shop of Mrs Watt who sold fish and later still became a fish and chip shop.

In this aerial view of 1930, Spence's Factory can be clearly seen in the middle, on the right. The streets which run upwards across this picture are from left to right: Torry Street continuing into Upperkirkgate, Littlejohn Street and Market Street continuing into Beachfield Street. Notice the Green Road between the fields on the right, which are now covered with houses. The street running from left to right in the foreground is King Street. Then bordering King Street is the Gordon Cleaning Company, built after the First World War by Alexander Christie who for fifteen years was Provost. The Cleaning Company closed down in 1984. On the site today is Somerfield's Supermarket.

Below opposite: The firm of William Spence and Son was for a long time one of the principal employers in Huntly and it came as a shock to Huntly folk when the firm closed down in 1990. An attempt made to revive the firm with a much reduced work force failed in 1993. The interior of Spence's Factory was decorated in May 1937 to celebrate the coronation of King George VI. The ladies are from left to right: Molly Knight, Nancy Cramb and Bunty Lyon.

Gordon Street terminates at the Market Street and Bleachfield Street intersection. In this 1987 photograph we see the well-known Huntly hostelry, the Lemon Tree, at the corner of Gordon Street and Market Street. This public house has called 'time gentlemen please!' for the last time. It has been converted into an Indian restuarant.

Just beyond the end of Gordon Street is Huntly Jubilee Hospital. In 1887 the people of the town raised enough money (more than £2,000) to build the hospital. This was deemed to be an excellent way to commemorate Queen Victoria's Jubilee. In this photograph taken around 1900 we can see the original building which now has extensive additions. In the background is the Binn.

By the beginning of the twentieth century the steam engine was not an uncommon sight in the Huntly area. This steam engine is doing the work of a dozen horses and is transporting a huge load of straw across the Market Muir around 1908. The canvas on the third cart proclaims the name of the firm 'Gray and Napier, Huntly.' Soon afterwards Alexander Gray set up in business on his own.

A number of the carts in the 1911 Coronation Parade were drawn by steam engines which had been hired from the contracting firm of Alexander Gray and Sons. Alexander 'Sandy' Gray is seen here carrying his son (also Alexander), and is standing beside one of his engines (a Garret named *Royal George*) which was about to take part in the parade.

The above photograph shows the contribution to the parade made by the Huntly joiners. Their cart is being pulled by a Marshall engine owned by Alexander Gray and Sons. On the roof of the cart is a portrait of King George V. In the photograph below we see the carts of the Huntly masons. The first cart contained men who worked with granite and the second cart those who worked with sandstone. At the engine's controls are John Hector and (John?) Robertson. In the 'granite cart' from left to right are: Frank Gordon, Bertie Duffus, Charlie Smith, Bob Mitchell, and Charlie and John Donald of Milton Farm. In the 'sandstone cart' are Peter Laing (left) and Willie Drummond.

Six

The New Feus

The New Feus comprises Gladstone Road, Albert Terrace and Richmond Road together with the shorter streets that traverse them at right angles, namely Victoria Road, Settrington Street and Queen Street. Settrington is the only one of these names that may require explanation. One of the many lesser titles held by His Grace the Duke of Richmond and Gordon, is that of Baron Settrington. The heir of the Duke is given the courtesy title of The Earl of March and Kinrara, and the Earl's heir is styled Lord Settrington. The building of houses in the area known as 'The New Feus' began in the last quarter of the nineteenth century.

During the last quarter of the nineteenth century, houses were built in the area which li
between Church Street and the River Bogie, and what came to be known as the 'New Feus.' I
1855, cows were grazing upon the fields that would one day become the New Feus. The Paris
Church sits atop the hill and the tower has still to be added to the Free Church.

In 1890 a man pushes his barrow up the Factory Brae. Behind him is a field upon which th
houses of Gladstone Road and of the yet non-existent Queen Street would be built. On th
right behind the gas lamp is part of Scott's Institution. The tall chimney belongs to th
Strathbogie Mill and overlooking the scene is the Battle Hill.

82

n 1855, with money bequeathed for the purpose by Alexander Scott of Craibstone, a hospital was built for the aged and infirm. Alexander Scott was a doctor who made his fortune in India and on his return to his native land bought the Craibstone Estate. The hospital, seen here in 1892, was a great asset to the town but was not large enough to cope with all the local people who desired to be admitted.

In 1900 another benefactor, Alexander Morrison of Bognie, left a substantial sum of money to Scott's Hospital (or to the 'Institution'). The money was used to enlarge the hospital. The camera has captured the building of the new west wing and the central tower that incorporates the main entrance. The new east wing seems well-nigh complete.

SCOTTS HOSPITAL, HUNTLY.

The completed building has the appearance of a large stately country house. In 1935 the railings were still in place but these were, of course, to be removed during the Second World War. The residents of Alexander Scott's Hospital are often entertained by local groups. Below is the Huntly Pipe Band who played in front of the building in 1967. The band members were from left to right, back row: Jimmy Horne, Colin Forsyth, John Gordon, James Grant, Robbie Innes, Forbes Milne, Ronnie Mitchell, Gordon Murray, George Neish, Clarence Gould, Johnston Aitken. Front row: Eric Dean, Billy Shand, Sandy Walker, Bill Dean, Billy McConnachie, Hamish Dean, Jimmy McConnachie, Brodie Ross, Derek Duncan.

From the tower of Scott's Institution can be seen an excellent view of the town. In 1935, Christ Church is completely obscured by trees, many of which have now been cut down. In the background is the Parish Church, while stretched below it are the three main streets of the 'New Feus', namely, Richmond Road, Albert Terrace and Gladstone Road. (PPC, Lilywhite)

From the tower we now look in the direction of the Clashmach. The gardens of the houses in the early years of the twentieth century lack the multitude of mature trees which they now possess. The large feus have now in many cases been divided up and additional houses built. Note in the middle the Bowling and Tennis Club with its original pavilion.

One of the many fine houses built in the New Feus is *Howglen* in Gladstone Road. It was built for the elderly Revd Robert Troup and his daughter Sophie. Robert Troup had married a cousin of the Huntly author George MacDonald, one of whose novels was named *Alec Forbes of Howglen*. From 1848 until 1876, Mr Troup had been the minister of Huntly Congregational Church. His daughter was blind and so the garden was planted with all sorts of fragrant flowers and herbs, and to this day on the house gate on Gladstone Road, the name *Howglen* is written in brail. This photograph has been produced from a magic lantern slide taken in 1899. Mr Troup is reading while Sophie pets the small dog sitting on her lap.

On the opposite side of the Bogie from the New Feus, stood MacDonald's Mill. The mill had formerly been owned by George and James MacDonald, father and uncle respectively, of the author. Meal was produced here from 1846 until it closed down in the early 1960s. In 1895 we see that the mill lacks the tower which was so familiar to later generations of Huntly people. The small cottage is thatched.

When meal production ceased in the 1960s, the mill soon fell into a state of dereliction. Latterly the mill had been owned by the firm of J.B. Yule and for many years meal had been supplied to prisons all over Britain. Walking away from the mill in 1984 are from left to right: Tom, Dorothy and Nan Pirie, along with dog 'Joncy.' Tom's father Sandy had for many years been head miller for J.B. Yule.

The winter of 1897 was severe and in many places the River Bogie was frozen over. MacDonald's meal mill was water-powered and in the winter, icy conditions sometimes prevented the mill wheel from turning and meal production had to stop until the thaw set in.

Seven
Churches

Prior to 1727, the people of Huntly had worshipped at Dunbennan and Kinnoir. When a new church was opened in Huntly in 1727, the kirks at Dunbennan and Kinnoir fell into disuse. A Catholic church dedicated to St John was built near Meadow Street in 1787 but was superseded by St Margaret's Church in 1834. The first Episcopal church separate from the Established Church was founded by the Revd Lewis Gordon in Gordon Street shortly after the 1715 rebellion, but was destroyed by Hanoverian troops in 1746. Strathbogie Church became Huntly's second Church of Scotland building in 1841 and two years later its congregation decided to join the Free Church of Scotland. The Congregational Church in Old Road sent missionaries to all parts of the world.

Dunbennan Kirk was for long the parish church of Huntly. Town folk as a consequence had to walk about two miles to attend services. In 1727 a church was opened in the town and Dunbennan was abandoned. Part of the old building was used to form an enclosure inside which is preserved a stone marking the burial place of George Chalmers, the minister of Dunbennan who died in 1626.

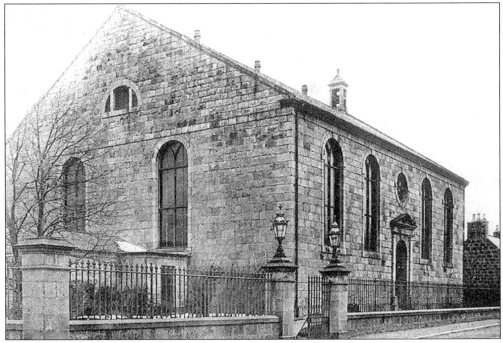

In 1805 the present church was built to replace the 1727 one that had become too small. The new kirk was if anything too large! It was designed to seat 1,800 people. The church in 1900 has altered little during the intervening one hundred years. The railings were removed during the Second World War, there are no longer lamps at the gates, and the weather vane in the form of a fish has not yet made its appearance atop the belfry.

In this aerial view of 1930, three of Huntly's churches can be seen: Huntly Parish Church, Strathbogie Parish Church and Christ Church. In Church Street are several buildings now demolished, for example, the 'Tanaree' and Deys' Engineering Works. In Princes Street on the left there are many vacant feus which are now built upon. Between Church Street and Princes Street is Sellar's factory, and on the right are Richmond Road and Victoria Road. The large gardens have now in many cases disappeared because of building. (Aerofilm Series)

The annual Sunday School picnic was an event that was looked forward to with great excitement by the children. The picnic was not held in some exotic location. Indeed, it was often held in the Show Park as was the case in 1926 when more than 600 Sunday Scholars of Huntly Parish Church and their teachers spent an enjoyable afternoon and evening there.

The Sunday School committee and staff of Huntly Parish Church in 1926 were from left to right, back row: Mr Clark, Miss Gray, Mr J. B. Summers, Miss Shirreffs, Miss E. Loggie, Mr Hynd, Miss Watson, Miss Henry, Mr G. Summers, Miss Howieson, Mr Eddie. Middle row: Mr Milton, Miss A. Gordon, Mr Mackenzie, Miss J. Loggie, Mr Donald, Mr Gray, Miss Alexander, Mr Mitchell, Miss Barclay, Mr Martin. Front row: Miss Smith, Mr Stephen, Miss Fraser, Mr Watt, Mrs Mackay, Revd A. Mackay, Mrs Watt, Mr Ironside, Miss Rhind, Mr Dickson, Miss McDonald.

The interior of the Parish Church has undergone some changes since 1925. Gone are the gas lamps, including the large central chandelier, and gone are the family pews with their tables and the gates leading to the pews. The plain windows were replaced with stained glass during the incumbency of the Revd Alexander Geddes.

Each November a Remembrance Day service is held in either Huntly or Strathbogie Church. Prior to this service, a short Act of Remembrance is held at the Memorial and then, led by the Pipe Band, the ex-servicemen and uniformed services march to the Kirk. Above, Huntly Pipe Band, leading the 1964 parade, is augmented with pipers from the 1st Huntly Boys' Brigade and has come to a halt outside the Parish Church.

Strathbogie Parish Church, the Congregational Church and St Margaret's can all be seen i
this 1925 panorama view from Scott's Hospital. The house with the large garden in th
foreground is the Rectory of Christ Church. Below is Strathbogie Parish Church around th
year 1900. A rough stone wall occupies the position where the Loggie building now stands.

The railings around the Congregational Church are on the right of this 1897 view of 'Golden Square.' This square has never received recognition as such and is officially regarded as part of Old Road. McVeagh Street, on the right, lost some of the old houses seen here with the building of the Good Templar Hall in 1908.

The Revd John Hill became minister of the Congregational Church in 1816 and soon afterwards formed a Sunday School for the young of the congregation. This was the very first Sunday School in Huntly. It proved extremely popular and members of other churches sent their children to it. At one time the total number of children taught in the Sunday School was almost 1,000. The children of the 1930 Sunday School are off to enjoy their annual picnic.

St Margaret's Church was opened in 1834, replacing St John's which had been built in 1787 by Charles Maxwell of Gibston. A great part of the funds required for the erection of the church came from the Gordon family of Wardhouse. The church is octagonal in shape and the beautiful facade is surmounted by an ornate spire which terminates in a crown and cross. In 1840, the Wardhouse family , by that time resident in Spain, presented the church with a fine altar piece and paintings. In recent years the church has been extensively restored. This engraving was sent in 1885 by James Robson, blacksmith, to John Brown, mason, both of Huntly.

The street leading from Deveron Street to St Margaret's has predictably been named Chapel Street. The view of the street in 1902 is hardly different from that of 1999. The long wall on the right has been pulled down to make way for additional houses.

In the severe winter of 1950, Chapel Street, like all the side roads of the town, was impassable due to the huge amount of snow that had fallen. The plough had cleared Deveron Street but George Street beyond was completely blocked. On the left is the store of William Hay & Sons, the lemonade firm.

The hairst of 1902 is underway in the field opposite St Margaret's. The houses of West Park Street and of Seton Drive now occupy this area. On the right of the church is the Catholic school, which was built in 1848 and ceased to be a school in 1969.

Christ Church, the Scottish Episcopal church, is the smallest of Huntly's churches and was built in 1851 in Provost Street. At that time there was in Huntly a second Episcopal church. This, however, followed the English liturgy. Christ Church is seen here on the fiftieth anniversary of its erection.

Eight

Leisure Time

The nineteenth century was a time when societies of an educational and recreational nature flourished. Many such as the Missionary Society and Men's Guild were church centred, and the Horticultural Society was encouraged by the Duchess of Gordon. The Field Club, founded in 1883, became very popular. Music and drama were well represented, while Freemasonry was revived and societies such as the Good Templars, Oddfellows and Rechabites were well attended. Cricket, which was said to resemble a local game called 'Stump the Loon', had an enthusiastic following. Golf, curling, bowls and tennis clubs were founded in the nineteenth century, and there was also a local football league. Unfortunately, many of these clubs are no longer with us. Fewer people now watch organised recreation and the coming of television has often been blamed for this change in attitude.

In 1908 the foundation stone of Loggie's Building was laid with masonic honours. Seated in the front of the company of more than seventy masons is Bro. William Loggie, and seated on his right is Bro. Alex Loggie. William Loggie's left shoulder is Past Master Bro. D. J. Mcpherson, next to whom is Past Master Bro. Joe Dunbar (with umbrella). On the latter's left, with top hat and light coat, is the Right Worshipful Master Bro. John Mitchell.

In 1904 the Freemasons bought the building which had formerly been St John's Catholic Church and this has been home to the Huntly Freemasons ever since. For many years a highlight of the local Masonic calendar was the celebration of the feast of St John. This frequently took the form of a dinner in the Lodge. The dinner in progress is that of 1916 or of 1917.

The Good Templars usually met in their hall in McVeagh Street. However, in 1912 they have congregated in the Castle Park in order to have their photographs taken. In the front row, seventh from the left, is Alex Gray. In the back row, eighth from the left, is Peter Gordon. The Templar Hall is now used by the Jehovah Witnesses.

Mr Bertie Diveri became organist of the Parish Church in 1894 and soon afterwards founded the town band of which he was conductor. On the 23 January 1900 a concert was held in Stewart's Hall in order to raise money for the Lord Lieutenant's Fund for wives and families of Aberdeenshire soldiers. Mr Diveri holds the baton. Also recognised is Tom Watt who took over as conductor a few years later. Mr Watt is on the extreme left of the second row from the back.

Above: Huntly had a band or orchestra until 1949 when, because of lack of interest, the orchestra was forced to close down. The funds remaining in the hands of the secretary of the orchestra were handed over to the Pipe Band. The band members of the late 1940s were from left to right, back row: Duncan Gordon, Lorna Fraser, -?-, Patrick McBoyle, George Donald. Front row: Jean Green, Willie Smith, Doris Bell, Jock Murdoch, Donald Duncan, Willie Cown, Bob Webster, Mr Spiers (Music Master, Gordon Schools), George Ross, Davie Duncan, Mattie Petrie, Tibbie Guthrie, Mary Christie, -?-, Tommy Pirie.

By 1960 the Harmonica Orchestra had raised in excess of £10,000 for charity, and guests at its concerts included Curly McKay, Jack Radcliffe and John Mearns. They also played in a BBC Country Music programme. The Harmonica Dance Band of the 1960s was composed of members of the Harmonica Band. They are from left to right: Willie Smith, Billy Green, Willie Scott, Bill Bews, Bill Stewart and Jean McConnachie(nee Munro).

Below opposite: The Huntly Harmonica Orchestra was formed in 1935 by Mr L. Gatherer. Its object was to raise money for charitable organisations. In 1938 the Orchestra won the band contest held in the Aberdeen Beach Ballroom. On that occasion the members were from left to right, back row: Sandy Davidson, Bud Littlejohn, Arthur Mollison (Drummer), Jack Sutherland, Jack Bowie. Third row: Jack Henderson, Alex Mollison (in evening suit), Jimmy Ross, Doddie Gibb, ? Dawson, Gordon Mitchell, Bill Smith, Phyllis Cormie, Sandy Lauder, Archie Shearer, Con Davidson, Bill Angus, Jerry Dawson, Bob Milne. Second row: Jim Wright, Tibbie Jessiman, Betty Jessiman, Willie (Tilly) Thomson, Gertie Jessiman, Margaret Jessiman, Sandy Keith. Front row: Donald Robertson, Sandy Forbes.

After the Second World War, Huntly Town Council decided that it would be good for the corporate morale to organise a Gala Week. The first of these was held from the 21 to the 26 July 1947. A Gala Queen and attendants were chosen and the crowning ceremony was performed by the Provost. From left to right: Lottie Florence, Provost McIver, Councillor Anderson, Ethel Morrison. Front: Mona McDonald, Helen Morrison, Evelyn Lockhart.

Drama featured largely in the life of the town from the 1880s until the 1960s. As part of Huntly's Coronation Festival in May 1953, the Gordon Schools Dramatic Society performed *The Neighbours* by Yves Cabrol. The players are from left to right, back row: Flora Higgins, William Thomson, Diana Barron, Tom Kennedy, Evelyn Lockhart. Front row: Gordon Sey, Dorothy Thomson.

The Huntly Operatic Society also used to be immensely popular. In 1934 the members performed *The Country Girl*. From left to right are: Patsy Duncan, Madge Gray, Peggy Watson, Dolly Boyd, Betty Mearns, Betty Lippe, Alastair Gordon, Eileen Donnelly, Bella Beange, Bella Duncan, Alice and Margaret Shewan, Emily Lippe, Minnie Gray.

A Boys' Brigade was founded in Huntly in 1897. It fell into abeyance in 1902 and wasn't revived until 1935. In 1938 the Boys' Brigade Pipe Band played at the Huntly Show, which was held in the Market Muir. From left to right, back row: Bill Jessiman, Stanley Munro, Dod McConnachie. Middle row: Ian McConnachie, Douglas Littlejohn, Sandy Fraser. Front row: William Oliver, Sandy Morrison, Derek Gordon.

Where there is piping, there is often Highland dancing. Such is the case in Huntly. In 1961, Betty Jessiman became World Champion Highland Dancer and was also awarded the MacLean Trophy for Champion of Champions. The Jessiman School of Dancing in McVeagh Street is well known throughout Scotland.

The Huntly Boy Scouts were formed in 1909 by Colour Sergeant Milton of the Volunteers. They fell into abeyance during the Great War, but at the end of hostilities were revived by Mr Summers, a PT master. A highlight of the Scout season was the annual summer camp. In 1935 the camp was held in the grounds of Cullen House. The boys at the notice board are from left to right: Sammy Morgan, Bill Bews, Jimmy Watt, Witham Burns, Norman Niven, Leslie Herbert, Jimmy Brown, Billy Pirie and Willie Whyte.

The group relaxing during Scout Camp Visitors' Day in 1936 are from left to right: Mrs Herbert, Mrs Law, Mr John Dickson, Mr Ian Law (Scoutmaster), Mr John Hunter (Scoutmaster), Leslie Herbert (Patrol Leader), Miss Bell Dickson, Andrew King (of Forgue), Mr Tom Herbert (English master at the Gordon Schools), and Mrs Dickson.

The Huntly Townswomen's Guild was formed in 1937 when there were 117 members. However, fifty years later the number had fallen to just twelve and it was decided to disband the organisation. The ladies at the final meeting are from left to right: Miss Rodger, Mrs Fyffe, Mrs Duncan, Mrs Carnegie, Mrs Gaiter, Mrs Aitken, Mrs Fraser, Mrs Gibb, Mrs Thomson, Miss McWilliam, Mrs Donald, Mrs Howard, Mrs Benzie, Mrs Murray (Chairman of North of Scotland Federation of Townswomen's Guilds).

Cricket was played in Huntly in the 1840s and the present club dates from 1854. To begin with, only friendly matches were played, but in 1889 Huntly participated in the newly formed Northern Cricket Association's Trophy Competition. In the final Huntly played Elgin Mechanics. The result was an easy win for Huntly. Batting first, Huntly scored 73 and in reply Elgin could muster a total of just 29. The victorious Huntly team are from left to right, back row: D. McGlashan, H.E. Spence, John Dey, J. Reid, G. Fraser Snr, Archie Rhind. Front row: W.S. Richardson, James Rhind, George Y. Jamieson, W.J. Gordon, Robert Macpherson.

All the members of the Cricket Club have gathered for this 1897 commemorative photograph. The following have been identified: Back row, fifth from left: Archie Rhind. Back row, seventh from left: Alex Dufton. Third row, on the left with striped blazer: T.A. Duff. Third row, third from left: John Scott. Third row, sixth from left: James Rhind. Third row, eighth from left: H.E. Spence. Third row, eleventh from left: John Rhind. Third row, twelfth from left: George Fraser Snr.

In the late 1980s the houses of Farquhar Road (next to the cricket park) were only partially built. This aerial view also includes the football park, the tennis courts and the golf course. It can be seen that the greater part of the golf course lies between the Rivers Deveron and Bogie. This area used to be called 'The Invers.'

Until extensive planting began in the 1980s, this gnarled ash (which had once been struck by lightening), was one of only a handful of trees growing in the Cooper Park. This card, sent during the First World War, shows sheep keeping the course in good trim for the golfers.

In the 1920s, Huntly Football Club often played their matches in a park which had for a long time been used by the proprietor of the Strathbogie Hotel on which to graze his horses. The park was known locally as the Strathbogie Park. (The name was changed to Christie Park in 1926). In this 1921/22 group, photographed in the Strathbogie Park are from left to right, back row: -?-. -?-, W. Shearer, -?-, Dod Laird, Willie Farquharson, Sandy Imlach, -?-, -?-. Middle row: Capt. Medhurst, -?-, Jim Thain, Jack Duncan, -?-, -?-, Alf Penny. Front row: Jock Chree, Charlie Maxwell, -?-. Capt. Medhurst was the club president.

110

One of the most successful of the local football teams was Muir United, who in 1936 won both the Lyon Cup and Usher Cup and were runners-up in the Wood Cup. From left to right, back row: Harry Knight, Sheema Sutherland, Jock Robertson, Jim Gordon, Davie Bain, Bill Barnett, Adam Black, Norman Connell, Jim Grant. Front row: Bill Simpson, Allan Gray, Alec Sey, Doddie Barnett, Eddie Watson.

Bowling in Huntly dates from 1881. In 1885 the bowlers moved to their present site in Richmond Road, where tennis was also catered for. This group of bowlers and tennis players have probably been photographed between the years 1892 and 1897, when James Bowman was Provost. Mr Bowman (bearded and white hatted) stands in the back row in front of the pavilion door. To the left of Mr Bowman is Joe Dunbar and to the right, T. A. Duff, who was for many years the Duke's factor.

Dr John O. Wilson was a patron of Huntly Bowling Club, who joined his father's practice in Huntly in 1878. He made his house calls on horseback and is remembered for not allowing even blizzards to deter him from visiting his country patients. 'Dr John' as he was often called, was one of the first men in Strathbogie to purchase a motor car. He died in 1946.

Huntly Rifle Club, which was formed in 1911, built an indoor shooting range for themselves in 1973 that was on ground which formerly had been part of the boys' playground of the primary school. The recipients of the Club trophies in 1960 or 1961 are from left to right: Abbie Rough, Peter Morrison, Fred Henderson, Jack Wishart, Harry Aitken, Gordon Robertson, John Scott, Bruce Farquhar and Harry Gordon

Nine
The Gordons

Huntly is the ancient capital of the Gordon Clan and the people of the town have always regarded the Gordon Highlanders as their own regiment. Duke Alexander was asked by the government in 1794 to raise a regiment of the line, and in this endeavour he was greatly helped by his wife Jane Maxwell, 'The Flooer o' Galloway.' It is said that she would favour each new recruit with a kiss and a shilling held between her teeth! On many occasions the Gordons have paraded through the town, and the regiment received the freedom of the Burgh in 1966. It was a sad day for the folk of Huntly when the Gordon Highlanders were amalgamated with the Queen's Own Highlanders in 1995.

In 1901 the drill hall was built for the Huntly Volunteers. One of the local 'bobbies' has crossed Deveron Street from the police station in order to appear in this photograph, attributed to Mr Bertie Diveri, the well-known organist.

Mr Peter Whyte, born in 1844, was a professional soldier who in due course became drill sergeant to the Huntly Volunteers. He was a keen freemason and it was in response to his motion that Lodge St John No. 745 was founded in 1883.

This group of young Huntly soldiers are enjoying a cup of tea after having been put through their paces by Drill Sergeant Summers, a veteran of the Boer War. The civilian in the background is Mr Joseph Dunbar of the *Huntly Express*. The officer is Major John Mitchell.

The First World War began one year and nine days after this photograph was taken, and many of these young men were destined to die in the trenches. On the extreme right is Bob Mitchell, who was killed. On the extreme left is Bertie Duffus, who survived.

Company Sergeant-Major Alexander Loggie was one of the 188 men of the Huntly district who were killed in the First World War. Sergeant-Major Loggie was the son of Alexander Loggie, stonemason, and of Mrs Loggie of No.36, Church Street. He had returned to this country in January 1918 for special training and then returned to the battlefields where he was killed in May.

In 1924 a large contingent of Gordon Highlanders took part in an arduous route march which took them through Huntly. The civilian watching them pass is Mr Hutcheon.

The sun is blazing down upon this Huntly crowd drawn up before the drill hall. The ladies are wearing large brimmed hats and several have parasols, but what is the occasion? Despite much investigation I still do not have the answer! The drill hall and the presence of soldiers suggest a military occasion. Notice the white-clad young ladies who seem to be selling flags. Major Dickson, Tom Duff, the Duke's factor, and Willie Morrison, Newton of Cairnie, have been identified.

In 1925, 'C' (Huntly) Company won the Battalion Championship Cup and the Cross Country Shield. From left to right, back row: Douglas Harper, Jimmy Thain, -?-, W. Allan, -?-, Charlie Duffus, -?-. Third row: Bill Lamont, Douglas Bowie, Bill Jamieson, -?-, -?-, Bill Bowie, -?-, -?-. Second row: -?-, Bob Buckley, Willie Castell, Lt Col. Murray Bisset, Jock Chree, Willie Rice, Bill Thain. Front row: Barney Beaghen, Jock Grant.

A high standard was maintained in 'C' Company and at another summer camp a few years later the Huntly men won the Battalion tug-of-war cup. Back row, on the extreme left: Jimmy Thain. Back row, second from left: Bob Shearer. Front row, second from left: Alec Gray. Front row, fourth from left: Alec Grant.

At the annual TA camp there was, of course, a battalion parade and it was an honour to be chosen to be part of the Colour Party. Second from the left is Huntly man Sergeant Jimmy Thain in this Colour Party from the mid-1920s.

The Second World War saw about 600 men from the Huntly area join HM Forces. In October 1939, Lt Col. Murray Bisset of Lessendrum led around fifty men down Bogie Street to the railway station. Provost Yule organised a collection which raised more than £30, and as a result 13,000 cigarettes were purchased and distributed among the men on the eve of their departure from Huntly.

Service men who were prisoners of war have gathered together in 1946 outside the Royal Oak, along with members of the 'Welcome Home' committee. From left to right, back row: J. Lobban, ? Gordon, George Robertson, B. Summers, ? Henderson, Bill Gordon. Middle row: -?-, ? Watt, J. Rough, J. Gordon, J. Neish, George Simpson, F. Bonner, W. Lobban, G. Hughes, J. Fraser, J. Sutherland. Front row: Harry Knight, Bill Pirie, J. Anton, Miss Yule, Provost McIver, Mrs Henderson, Charlie Anderson, R. Dufton, -?-.

On 6 June 1966, the Gordon Highlanders, with bayonets fixed, drums beating and colours flying, marched through the Square after having received the freedom of the burgh. Provost William Watson takes the salute while Baillie Charlie Smith takes a souvenir photograph of the occasion. The parade is led by Lt Col. Neish.

The Gordons were regular visitors to the town. In 1981 the Regimental Band entertained the local people by 'beating retreat' in the Square. In the background a football match is in full swing in the Christie Park. On 27 June 1994, the Gordons had their freedom of the Burgh confirmed. Unfortunately, in 1995 the Government in a penny-pinching exercise decided to amalgamate the Gordon Highlanders with the Queen's Own Highlanders. (PPC, Huntly Express)

Ten
Landward

Huntly is the centre of a rich agricultural area that formerly was entirely the property of the Gordon family. From the time of Duke Alexander there was a tendency for small holdings to be amalgamated into larger farms. However, this was done in a humane manner. There were no 'clearances' on Gordon lands. Huntly was (and still is) the market town for the area and extensive forests are to be found in the vicinity of the town. In 1839 the Duke of Richmond and Gordon planted 2,258 acres of the Binn with trees, giving employment to many when work was hard to get. Since 1839 the area planted with trees has been considerably added to.

Huntly is the centre of a large agricultural area and for at least 500 years it has been a market town. Markets at one time were held in the Square and in the Market Muir. In 1896 it was decided that the town should have an auction mart and a field behind the railway station was chosen for that purpose. The mart in due course became the property of Aberdeen and Northern Marts Ltd, and this company in 1990 decided to close down Huntly Mart and replace it with a new mart in Inverurie. However, in 1992 local farmers opened a new Huntly Mart near the bypass below the Ward. In the above illustration, sheep are penned outside the old Mart in readiness for the 1955 Spring Sale, while below, the sale is in full swing with Charlie Macdonald acting as auctioneer.

The wool of the sheep would at one time have been woven into blankets at the Richmond Mills. These were situated on the River Bogie about quarter of a mile from Macdonald's Mill. These three men and three women would have been the mill's entire workforce around 1895, each carrying the tools of his or her trade. One man displays a tartan blanket made at the mill.

Richmond Mills were for many years owned by the Brander family. Charlie Brander (left) and Jock Grant are working at a machine that spun two-ply wool and wound it on to bobbins, each of which weighed one pound. When Charlie Brander retired in 1979, the last water-powered mill in the Huntly district closed. The mill has since been demolished.

The milkman with his horse and cart used to be a familiar sight in every town and village in the land. Two local dairy farms were Milton of Castleton, and Piriesmill. *Above:* Norman (left) and Maxie Donald (sons of the owner of the Milton Dairy) are helping milkman Dod Whyte and horse 'Duncan' make their deliveries in West Park Street in 1928. *Below:* Pirriesmill's large Belgian horse 'Dobbin' waits patiently for his round to begin. The milkman is George Dow and by his side is Jock Fowler. The two boys in this 1941 group are George Dow Jnr and a friend who had been evacuated from Glasgow.

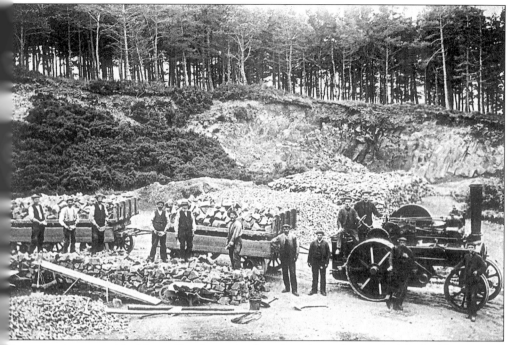

Steam engines were ideal for pulling heavy loads such as the rocks required for building or road making. The men of Cruichie Quarry in Drumblade were no doubt happy for a break in their hard work while they had their photograph taken. The time is reckoned to be around the year 1900.

These two five ton steam wagons at Glendronach Distillery were owned by Alexander Gray of Huntly. On the left is No. 33854, a 'Garret', which was new in 1920. On the right is No. 33719, which was originally with the city of Dundee and bought by Mr Gray in 1931. The men are from left to right: C. Stephen, Alex Gray Jnr, -?- and J. Simpson.

Many farms and crofts have disappeared during the course of the twentieth century. Most have been absorbed into larger agricultural units. 'The Queels' is typical of the small crofts in the parish of Huntly which are no more. The ruins of the Queels are to be found surrounded by thick woodland off the Huntly-Dufftown road. Seen at the Queels in happier times in the late 1890s are from left to right: Sandy Grant, Mary Grant, Elsie Grant, -?- and Sandy Spence.

Under the jurisdiction of the Huntly Postmaster were several sub-post offices (thirty-five in the 1960s). These included Ruthven Post Office, seen here in 1933. Members of the Watt family who ran the post office stand at the doorway. It was one of the last buildings in the district to retain its thatched roof and ceased to be a post office in the 1950s.

The farm of Dunbennan lies next to Dunbennan Kirkyard. Employed to look after the Kirkyard was Sandy Grant, and he has been invited across to the farm to have his photograph taken (in the early 1920s), along with the farm servants who were busy threshing. Sandy is third from the right. The farmer, Mr Wilson, has also turned up and is second from the left.

Huntly has enjoyed a good supply of piped water since 1866. In the 1930s, however, the Town Council decided that more water was required and that a dam should be built. The first sod cut in connection with the dam's construction was made by Provost Alexander Christie. Looking on, from left to right are: Mr Allardice, Mr Dufton (grocer) and Mr Sandy Gray (all wearing hats). Behind the Provost, also wearing hats, are Mr Norman Yule and Mr Jim Yule. To the right of the flag are Mr McIver (winged collar), Mr Alex Lobban (spectacles) and Mr Frank Stephen (hands in pockets). The dam was completed in 1937.

The extensive afforestation in the hinterland of Huntly has for the last 150 years provided employment for a good number of Huntly men. Dan and Archie Lockhart were timber merchants who had several sawmills including one in the Binn. Of this 1919 group, only Andy Paterson (fourth from the left) has been identified. Andy, who was about fourteen years old, was employed as a 'picker loon.'

'The Closing Day, Huntly' is the name given to this scene viewed from the Battle Hill sometime before the First World War. (PPC, H. McConachie)